Danebridge started the game in great style. After mounting a series of dangerous attacks, the Reds put the ball in the Selworth net.

'What a goal!' cried Rakesh. 'Keeper never moved!'

His delight was short-lived. He'd just leapt onto the scorer's back, toppling Ryan to the ground, when the referee's repeated blasts on the whistle made him realize something was wrong.

'No goal,' announced Selworth's teacher . . .

Published by Corgi Yearling Books:

SOCCER MAD
ALL GOALIES ARE CRAZY
FOOTBALL DAFT
FOOTBALL FANATIC
FOOTBALL FLUKES
SOCCER STARS
THE SOCCER MAD COLLECTION
(*includes Soccer Mad/All Goalies are Crazy*)
SOCCER AT SANDFORD
SANDFORD ON TOUR

Published by Corgi Pups,
for beginner readers:

GREAT SAVE!
GREAT SHOT!

ROB CHILDS

THE

BIG DROP

Illustrated by Aidan Potts

YOUNG CORGI BOOKS

The rig̲ ̲ ̲ ̲ s work
has been asserted in accordance with the Copyright, Designs and
Patents Act 1988

Set in 14/18pt New Century Schoolbook by
Phoenix Typesetting, Ilkley, West Yorkshire

Young Corgi Books are published by Transworld Publishers Ltd,
61–63 Uxbridge Road, Ealing, London W5 5SA,
in Australia by Transworld, c/o Random House Australia Pty Ltd,
20 Alfred Street, Milsons Point, NSW 2061, Australia,
and in New Zealand by Transworld Publishers, c/o Random House
New Zealand, 18 Poland Road, Glenfield, Auckland, New Zealand.

The Random House Group Limited supports The Forest Stewardship
Council® (FSC®), the leading international forest-certification organisation.
Our books carrying the FSC label are printed on FSC®-certified paper.
FSC is the only forest-certification scheme supported by the leading
environmental organisations, including Greenpeace. Our
paper procurement policy can be found at
www.randomhouse.co.uk/environment

Printed and bound in Great Britain by Clays Ltd, St Ives plc

For all young Asian footballers

1 Relegation Battle

'No sweat!' exclaimed Rakesh. 'All we have to do is beat Ashford and we'll be OK, look!'

'I'm trying to, if you'd shift out the way a bit so the rest of us can see,' said Chris, shuffling for position among the footballers clustered around the sports noticeboard.

The latest league table did not make happy viewing for Chris Weston, neither as goalkeeper nor team captain of Danebridge Primary School.

It gave him a painful reminder that he had already let in 28 goals this season. And it also showed Danebridge in the wrong half – third from bottom out of nine schools.

					Goals		
League table – bottom three . . .							
	P	W	D	L	F	A	Pts
Danebridge	13	3	3	7	19	28	12
Brentway	14	2	4	8	16	35	10
Ashford	14	2	3	9	20	37	9

'At least we still have three matches left to play,' put in Philip, who was tall enough to study the table from the back of the group. 'The others have only got two.'

'Just as well,' Chris muttered. 'We might need that game in hand, if we go

and mess things up against Ashford tomorrow.'

'We won't do that,' Rakesh assured him. 'Anyway, even getting one more point from a draw would be good enough to make us safe – right?'

'Well, just about, but not mathematically.'

'You sound like the Professor,' chuckled the striker, referring to a teammate who was also a genius with

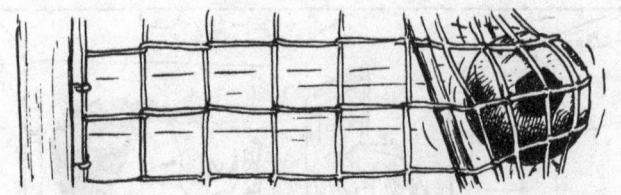

numbers – something Rakesh would never pretend to be. 'I thought we had a better goal difference than Ashford.'

'We do – but if they had a big win, everything could change.'

'Good job only one team goes down, then, I reckon,' said Philip.

'Yeah, so long as it's not us who end up getting the chop.'

Danebridge's headmaster gathered the players together before the kick-off at Ashford next day.

'It's up to you,' he stressed. 'Your fate's in your own hands – and feet.'

Mr Jones didn't bother to mention their heads. He could barely recall anyone scoring a headed goal apart from Philip, in a cup match.

'You've done very well to recover after losing the first four games of the season,' he praised them. 'Another three points for a victory today and you can forget any relegation fears.'

Rakesh started the match as if he intended to win it all by himself. For a time, it was almost a one-man show.

Danebridge's leading scorer fired in four shots on target in quick succession. He hit the goalkeeper once, the woodwork twice and finally found the net with a crisp half-volley from the edge of the penalty area.

Only then did he allow somebody else in on the act – a girl. Rakesh swept across a perfect centre for his strike

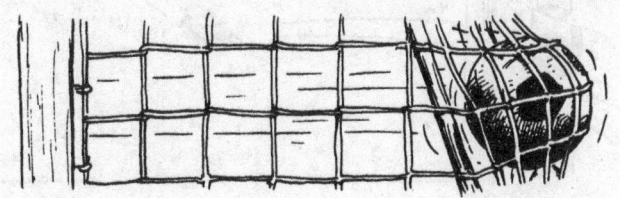

partner to slide home the second goal at the far post. All Kerry had to do was tap the ball over the line.

'Thanks, Rakky,' she smiled, jumping up to slap his raised hand in celebration. 'You put it on a plate for me. I couldn't miss.'

'Plenty more where that came from,' he grinned. 'This lot are useless. No wonder they're bottom of the league.'

The shock of going 2–0 down in this vital relegation battle seemed to wake Ashford up. Either that or the Danebridge players dozed off in the spring sunshine, dreaming of helping themselves to a feast of goals whenever they felt hungry.

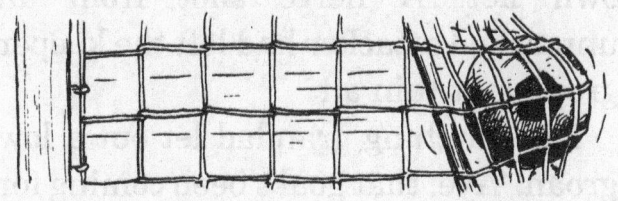

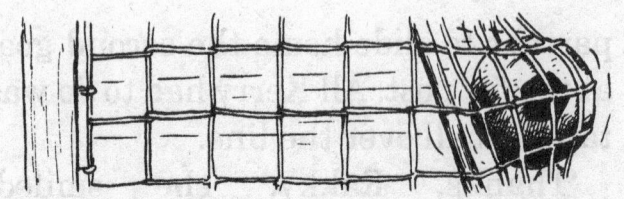

As Danebridge eased up, they failed to heed the danger signs that the home side were beginning to find their form and putting together some promising moves. Even after Chris had been forced to make an acrobatic save, the captain's anxious warnings fell upon deaf ears.

'C'mon, team, get a grip!' he urged. 'We're giving them too much space.'

It came as no surprise to the spectators when a grumbling Chris soon had to fish the ball out of the back of his own net. A fierce shot from an unmarked attacker had left the keeper groping at thin air.

His watching grandad let out a low groan. 'Aye, that goal's been coming for a while. I could feel it in my aching bones.'

Mr Jones nodded sadly. 'If we're not careful, we're going to throw this match away.'

The headmaster changed the team formation during the interval, using two substitutes, but it was to no avail. The second half was a total disaster.

It began in dramatic fashion with penalties at both ends.

Tripped as he was about to shoot, Rakesh insisted on taking the penalty himself and blazed the kick wildly over the crossbar. Two minutes later, the Professor handled the ball in attempting to clear a corner and the referee pointed to the spot again.

Unfortunately, Chris didn't have the luxury of seeing the ball sail over the bar. Ashford's penalty was aimed low for the bottom left-hand corner of his goal. He guessed correctly and dived full-length, but the kick had too much power. It brushed past his outstretched arm to level the scores at 2–2.

After that, things went from bad to worse. Danebridge wasted several chances to regain the lead before conceding a soft third goal against the run of play.

Ashford's number nine bustled through Philip's clumsy challenge and shot from a narrow angle, off balance. The ball took a slight deflection off another defender's boot and somehow squeezed over the line between Chris and his near post. It proved a costly error.

At the final whistle, the dejected captain made a brave effort to call out 'Three Cheers' for their opponents, but the response from his teammates was half-hearted. They knew they had blown it – and also that they had only themselves to blame for the disastrous 3–2 defeat.

As the Danebridge players trudged

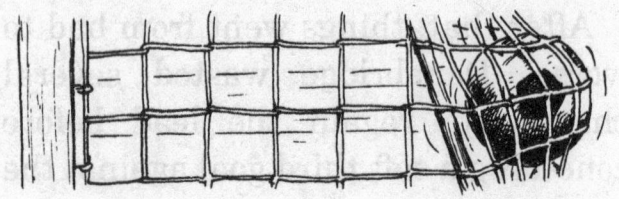

off the pitch, they tried to avoid looking one another in the eye. They were too busy staring relegation full in the face.

2 Ups and Downs

'Knew you lot would go down this season without me in the team.'

Rakesh ignored the voice behind him in the lunch queue and carried on discussing the match. 'If only I'd scored that penalty, the result might have been different.'

'Not your fault we lost. I'd have been too nervous even to take it,' admitted Philip.

'Guess that's why I missed it. I knew how much was at stake . . .'

He was interrupted again. 'The reason you missed it, Patel, was 'cos you're rubbish!'

Rakesh turned round to confront Luke Bradshaw. 'What's it got to do with you? Nothing!'

Luke smirked at them. 'Got some news you might like to hear.'

'Doubt it.'

'Do you want the good news or the bad?'

'Is the good news that you're leaving?' asked Philip cheekily. Although he was a year younger than Luke, he was already taller, and felt safe that the bully would think twice about taking him on.

'No such luck,' Luke sneered. 'Wish I could get out of this dump and go somewhere that recognized my talents.'

Luke had never forgiven the headmaster for banning him from playing football for the school after causing trouble earlier in the season.

'Didn't know you had any talents,' said Rakesh, deliberately goading him. The two of them barely spoke to one another usually, apart from trading insults.

'Don't push yer luck, Patel,' snarled Luke, his fists clenching. 'Bet you didn't know either that Brentway won yesterday as well.'

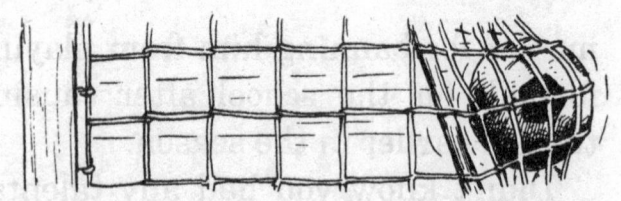

'I don't believe you. You're just making it up.'

Luke shrugged. 'Suit yourself. I know a kid who goes there. Perhaps you'll believe dear old Jonesy when he gets round to tellin' you.'

'So what's the good news, then?' asked Philip as Luke moved off to push in the queue nearer the front.

'That *is* the good news, stupid,' he called back over his shoulder. 'At least to me it is. It means you're now level bottom with Ashford.'

He began to taunt them with a tuneless chant, annoying everyone else around him too. '*Goin' down . . . goin' down . . . goin' down . . .*'

*

After school, Chris kept a weekly date with Kerry – on horseback!

At the start of term, the captain had found a way to persuade sharpshooter Kerry to play for the school team. He bet her that she couldn't score goals in a proper football match like she did every Monday afternoon in Games. She took up the challenge and he lost the bet – both as expected.

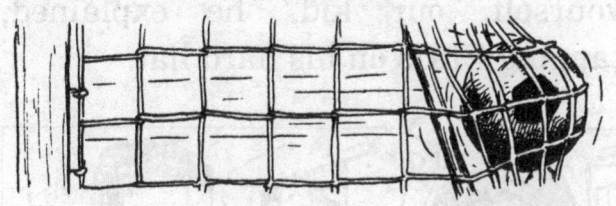

Today was the day for Chris to fulfil his side of the bargain – that he would learn to ride well enough to attempt a jump. Time was running out for him to do so. The team was still recovering from the shock of hearing that Kerry would be leaving soon. Her parents were going to open a new riding school in another county.

The event was drawing a crowd. Several of the players turned up to watch, and so had Grandad and Chris's older brother.

Andrew had come straight from school, still in the uniform of Selworth Comprehensive. 'Couldn't miss the chance of seeing you make a fool of yourself, our kid,' he explained, tapping Chris on his hard hat.

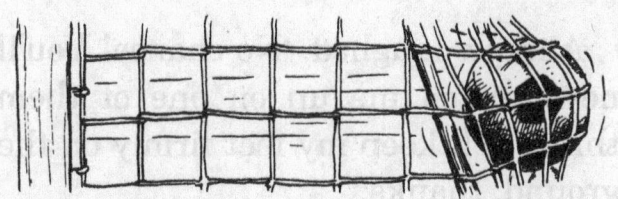

Chris pulled a face. 'Should've known. You have a habit of popping up at just the wrong time.'

'Charming! And here's me ready to run to your rescue,' he sniggered. 'I've brought a load of safety pins and Sellotape to stick you back together again after you fall off!'

'Don't hold your breath. Kerry says there's nothing to it. The pony does most of the work.'

Andrew gazed towards the stables. 'Which one's yours? That great big black brute?'

'No, the little chestnut.'

'Ah! How sweet!' Andrew cooed sarcastically. 'My little pony.'

'I'd like to see you ride it.'

Andrew laughed. 'No chance! You'll never catch me up on one of them things. I'll keep my feet firmly on the ground, thanks.'

'Well, then, you shouldn't mock,' said Grandad. 'Chris has done very well in just a few lessons.'

'I was dead nervous when I first got on,' Chris admitted, 'but riding's great fun. Might decide to keep it up, even after Kerry's gone.'

He discovered that Kerry's mother, the instructor, was taking his group of beginners on a short hack around a couple of fields before returning to the school paddock to practise jumping. Kerry went with them to help, riding her favourite palomino pony.

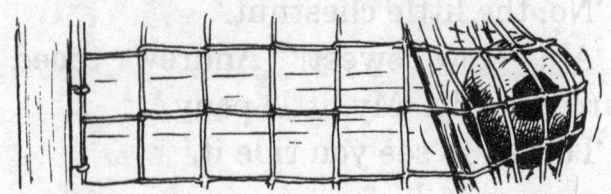

As they changed from a walk to a trot, Kerry moved up alongside Chris. 'Relax, keep well balanced,' she advised. 'Feel the rhythm, sit and rise, sit and rise – that's it, good.'

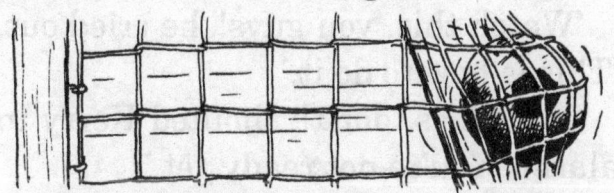

Chris grinned. 'Think I might be catching this riding bug, just like you've done with soccer.'

'At least it takes your mind off relegation for a while.'

'Right – the only big drop I'm worried about at the moment is falling off when we start jumping.'

'Falling doesn't bother me,' Kerry said with a laugh. 'It's hitting the ground that hurts!'

As the ponies completed a circuit of the first field, they broke into a canter.

Seeing Andrew and the others leaning against the fence, Chris felt a sudden surge of bravado. He noticed an old rotten log lying in the grass not far away and turned towards it.

'Watch this, you guys!' he cried out. 'This is how to do it.'

'No, Chris, don't!' shouted Kerry in alarm. 'You're not ready yet.'

It was too late. Chris could not have stopped the pony now even if he'd wanted to – which he did. His confidence of a few moments ago had totally deserted him.

He did the right thing by instinct, leaning forward as the pony jumped the log, but failed to straighten up again on landing. The jolt threw him further forward, his feet came out of the stirrups and he lost hold of the reins too. Chris grabbed the pony's mane to try and save himself, then

wrapped his arms around its neck and clung on for all he was worth. Within a few strides, however, he slid down one side and was bumped off into the long grass.

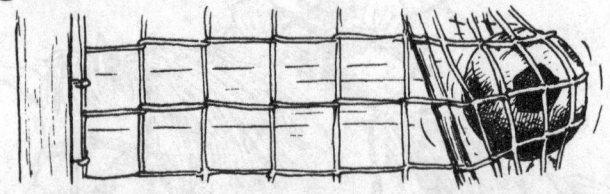

Kerry was the first to reach him, dismounting quickly to check that he was all right. Chris was too winded to speak and had no defence against her scolding tongue once she was sure there was no damage done.

'Idiot! What did you go and do a crazy thing like that for?' she complained. 'Showing off in front of your mates. Typical!'

Andrew only just beat Grandad over the fence and they arrived on the scene as Chris was getting shakily to his feet. 'Didn't know that was how it was supposed to be done, little brother,' he teased.

'It's not,' Kerry snapped. 'He's just taking after his big brother for a change – acting stupid!'

'Oh dear! She's cross. You won't get a gold star now, our kid,' he grinned as Kerry sprang up into her saddle.

'Well, c'mon, then,' she ordered. 'No good feeling sorry for yourself. Mum's got your pony so go and get back on. The lesson's not over yet.'

Grandad was rather more sympathetic and helped Chris to brush himself down. 'Looks like you've learnt one thing already, m'boy,' he said with a chuckle.

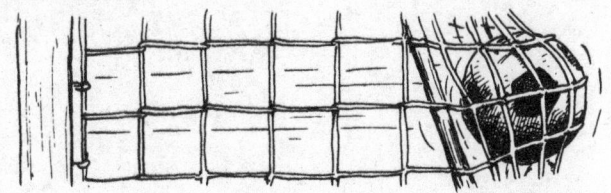

'What's that, Grandad?' he said sheepishly.

'The truth of the old saying: *Pride comes before a fall*!'

Chris nodded. 'I think we all found that out for ourselves in the Ashford match,' he said, sighing. 'And now I'll be making doubly sure we won't make that kind of mistake again.'

3 *Seeing Red*

'Good save, Rakky!' cried Kerry. 'We'll have to play you in goal next game.'

Rakesh grinned. He was well pleased with the stop he'd just made to prevent her scoring. 'Nah , think I'll let Chris keep his job. He's a better goalie than he is a show-jumper!'

Making jokes at the captain's expense had given them all plenty of laughs over the past few days, but Chris took the ribbing in good heart. In a funny sort of way, it seemed to have

helped lift everyone's spirits again after the Ashford defeat.

Kerry didn't normally join in the lunchtime kickabout with the other footballers. She preferred to play with her own friends. But she found herself increasingly caught up with the team's efforts to do the double – to escape relegation and win the Cup. Danebridge still had a semi-final game to look forward to and Kerry was keen to reach the Final, even if she would not be around after Easter to take part in it.

As the action switched to the other end of their short pitch where Chris was in goal, Rakesh didn't see Luke sidle up behind him.

'Fancy yourself as a keeper, do you?' came the sneering remark.

'Not really,' Rakesh replied with a heavy sigh. 'Just taking my turn.'

Luke kicked out in spite at the cast-off clothes that made up one of the posts, scattering them about.

'Clear off, will you,' Rakesh snapped, rebuilding the pile. 'You know we don't want you here.'

'Huh! Put you off, do I? Just 'cos you all know I'm the best player in the school.'

'There's only you who thinks that. We lost every game you played in.'

'That was stupid old Jonesy's fault, not mine. He should never have picked Weston as captain.'

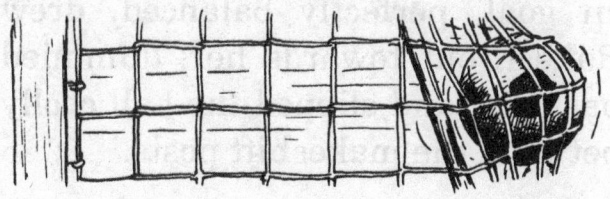

'Good decision, if you ask me.'

'I'm not askin' you,' Luke scoffed. 'Look what's happened without me. Things are so bad, Jonesy's even had to start pickin' girls!'

'Belt up, Bradshaw,' Rakesh said wearily, tired of such a pointless argument. 'Kerry's a great goal-scorer. If you can't see that, you must be blind.'

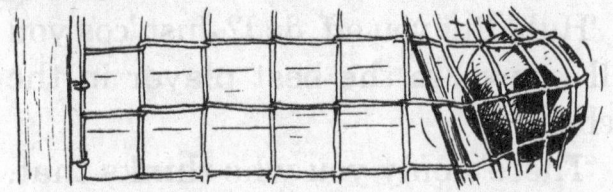

Just at that moment, as if intent on proving his point, Kerry broke away with the ball. She kept it under full control as she advanced rapidly on goal, perfectly balanced, drew Rakesh out towards her, dummied past him and slipped the ball coolly between the makeshift posts.

'Anybody else want to go in goal?' Rakesh shouted out. 'There's a bad smell hanging round there.'

Something flew past his head. He didn't know whether it was a stone or a piece of dirt. He whirled round to confront his tormentor.

'Watch it! You do that again and I'll . . .'

'You'll do what?' Luke cackled. 'Accuse me of racism?'

'The colour of my skin's got nothing to do with it,' Rakesh fumed.

'Oh, yeah? Well, this is what I think of you people then . . .'

Luke began to spout a torrent of racial abuse aimed at Rakesh and his family. The next thing the players knew, Rakesh had launched himself at Luke and the two boys were wrestling on the ground.

'Fight! Fight!' went up the shout.

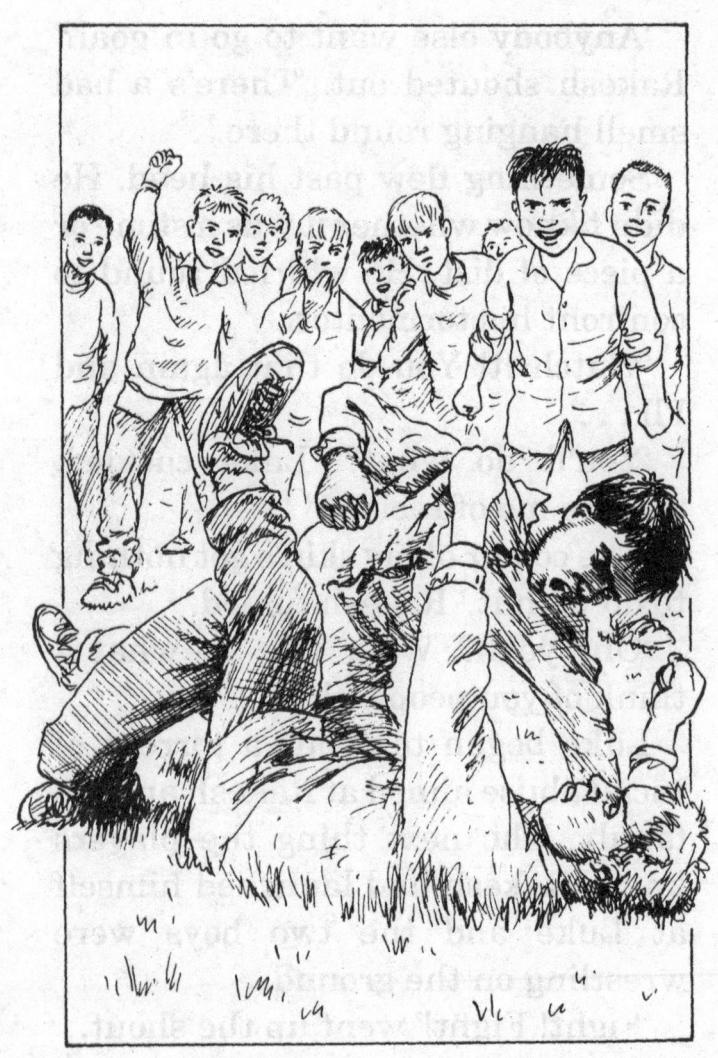

The pummelling pair immediately attracted a large group of onlookers, all circling around them to get a better view. By the time Chris arrived, there was already blood splattered about, but it wasn't clear whose nose or mouth it was coming from.

'C'mon, help me,' Chris cried out. 'We've got to break it up.'

Philip waded in with the captain to try and pull the fighters apart and a wayward fist thumped Chris on the shoulder. Two lunchtime supervisors dashed up to put a stop to the free-for-all and sent six children, including Kerry, into school to see the headmaster.

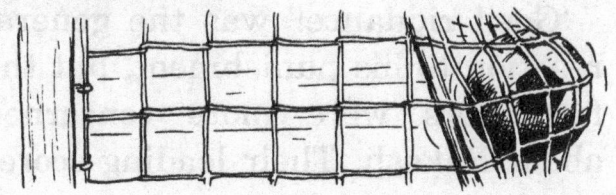

'Going at it like a bunch of wild hooligans, they were,' one of the women reported to Mr Jones.

'And such terrible language too,' added the other.

'Right, thank you, ladies,' he said grimly. 'This is a very serious matter. Just leave it to me now. I'll deal with it.'

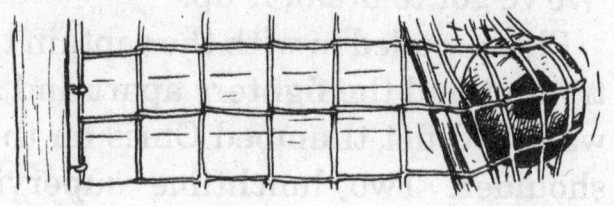

Luke Bradshaw was sent home in disgrace and also suspended from school for the rest of term.

'Good riddance!' was the general reaction to his punishment, but the footballers were more concerned about Rakesh. Their leading scorer had been dropped from the next league fixture, Danebridge's crucial last home match of the season.

'I don't think it's fair,' said Chris that evening in Grandad's cottage, telling him about what had happened. 'I mean, Jonesy knows why the fight started. Kerry spoke up for Rakesh. She heard what Bradshaw said to him.'

'Nasty piece of work, that Luke Bradshaw, by all accounts,' replied Grandad. 'The boy may well find himself in more hot water yet over this business, but your headmaster was in an awkward position today. He could hardly have let Rakesh off scot-free, however bad the provocation.'

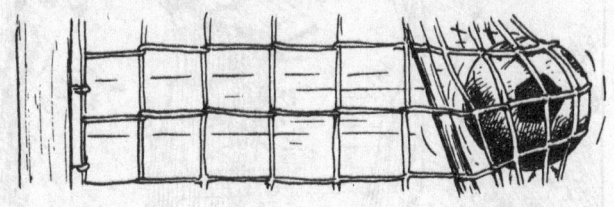

Chris pulled a face. 'Well, Jonesy won't be able to complain if we go and lose now after banning his main striker.'

'Football's a team game,' said Grandad. 'Rakesh isn't the only one who can put the ball in the back of the net, you know. It gives other people a chance now to show what they can do.'

Chris didn't seem convinced. 'I just can't stand the thought of Luke going around bragging that he helped to get us relegated.'

'You'll be OK, m'boy,' Grandad assured him. 'Sounds to me like that's all the motivation the team will need to do well against Highgate.'

'Hope you're right. We've already won 2–0 away at their place so they'll be out for revenge.'

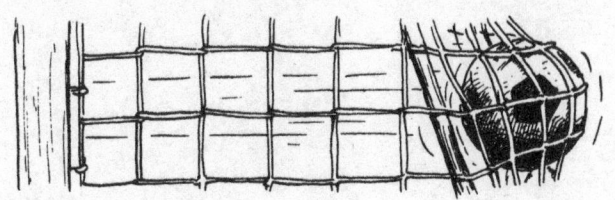

4 *Three's a Crowd*

'C'mon, the Reds!' cried Rakesh as the striped shirts of Danebridge kicked off against the all-white strip of Highgate Juniors.

Rakesh was among the spectators, eager to play a part by cheering the team to a victory that would put them three points clear of Ashford again. His one consolation in missing this game – apart from giving Luke Bradshaw a black eye – was that at least he'd be able to play on Saturday at Selworth, his previous school. He was desperate to do well against his old mates.

Grandad did not have far to travel to see his favourite team in action – just a short walk down his garden path on to the village recreation ground. He soon sensed how nervous the players must be feeling. They could barely string two passes together.

'Good job we're not up against a better team than Highgate, by the look of things,' Grandad grunted to himself. 'They're just as bad as we are.'

It was certainly not the best game that he had ever watched on the recky. If it had been on television, he would have either switched over, turned off or gone to sleep. The dismal first half proved goal-less, but that situation changed immediately after the restart.

A miskick in midfield and poor marking in defence allowed a Highgate attacker a clear run at goal. Chris came out to narrow the shooting angle, but the ball was lobbed over his head and just underneath the crossbar.

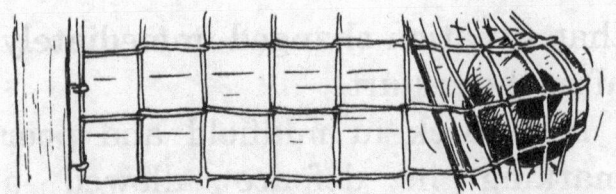

As Chris trailed back to scoop the ball out of the netting, he noticed a figure saunter over the footbridge across the River Dane. 'Oh, great, that's all we need,' he groaned. 'Bradshaw's come to gloat.'

Luke checked the score with a spectator before stopping behind the goal. 'Losin', are we?' he smirked. 'What a shame!'

'Didn't think you'd dare show your ugly face here,' Chris replied.

'Huh! Jonesy can't stop me comin' on the recky. Nobody can.'

'You want a bet on that?' said Chris, nodding at another newcomer who suddenly appeared at Luke's side.

'Time to go home, I reckon, Bradshaw.'

The harsh voice made him jump.

'I only just got here,' he protested.

'So have I. And you know what they say – three's a crowd . . .'

Luke took the hint. He slouched away back to the bridge without even making any other snide comments to annoy Chris. He could tell the older boy meant business.

'. . . and two's company, eh? Just you and me now, our kid.'

'Thanks, Andrew,' Chris smiled. 'I take back what I said last week. You timed your arrival just right for once.'

Andrew smirked. 'Anything else I

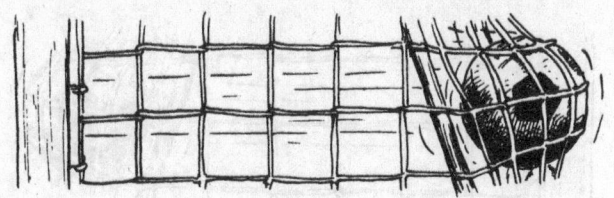

can do for my little brother? I've got my boots with me if you need a supersub.'

'Sorry, we'll have to manage without you somehow. You're too old!'

'Yeah, guess their teacher might object,' Andrew laughed. 'But Jonesy must be wishing he could bring Rakky on now, eh?'

Rakesh was doing his best to help. He'd spent the whole match shouting advice and encouragement.

'Play it wide, Professor,' he screamed as Danebridge launched an attack in search of the equalizer. 'Give it to Ryan. He's got loads of space.'

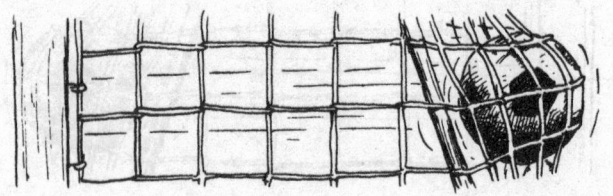

Mark Towers, alias the Professor, must have heard him. Or perhaps it was simply his boots obeying their master. The absent-minded Professor had left his own at home – not for the first time – and had borrowed Rakesh's pair.

Ryan was running free along the right touchline and took Mark's pass in his stride. The young winger had time to look up and pick out a target for his cross, spotting just the one he wanted – Kerry.

His centre wasn't as accurate as he might have liked, though, and Kerry had to check back to gain possession. It allowed a defender to charge down her delayed shot and the ball rebounded out of the danger area. Or at least that's what the Highgate goalkeeper thought.

Mark had wandered forward in

support of the attack and the ball sat up perfectly for him, almost begging to be hit. So he granted its wish and walloped the ball as hard as he could. It flew out of the keeper's reach and snicked the inside of the post on its way into the net.

'Magic boots, Rakky!' he cried, waving across to him.

Rakesh grinned. 'Bradshaw might have got me banned, but he couldn't stop my boots from scoring!'

The last ten exciting minutes made up for the rest of the drab match as Danebridge pressed hard for the winning goal. Kerry went closest with a volley that skimmed over the bar, although Ryan might have grabbed the glory for himself if he'd kept a cooler head. His hurried shot was poked tamely straight at the goalkeeper.

In the end, Danebridge had to be grateful that their captain stayed alert and on his toes. Chris had to sprint from his area to snuff out the threat of a late Highgate raid by kicking the ball away almost into the river.

The 1–1 draw gave the Reds a precious point, but their relief was only temporary. The next day, they were dismayed to see on the notice-board that Brentway remained above them in the league table. It was clear that any of the bottom three schools could still be relegated.

	P	W	D	L	Goals F	A	Pts
Brentway	16	3	5	8	20	38	14
Danebridge	15	3	4	8	22	32	13
Ashford	15	3	3	9	23	39	12

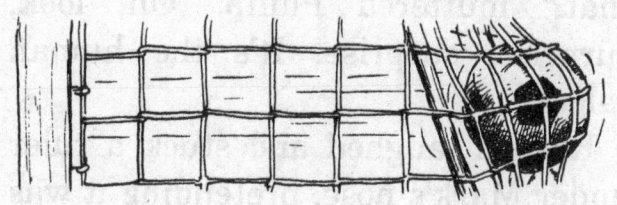

'Brentway must have got a draw too,' Philip groaned.

'Yeah, but they've run out of games,' said Rakesh. 'They can only sweat it out now, hoping that either us or Ashford slip up.'

'Who are Ashford playing?'

It was Chris that answered. 'Highgate at home, so we can't rely on that lot doing us any favours. I bet Ashford will beat them, just like we should have done.'

'It all comes down to mathematics,' piped up a voice behind them. 'Most things do in the end.'

'Now I wonder who could have said

57

that?' muttered Philip. 'Oh, look, surprise, surprise! It's the human calculator!'

Rakesh laughed and stuck a ruler under Mark's nose, pretending it was a microphone. 'We're lucky to have the Professor here in the studio, listeners. Perhaps he can explain the situation to us. Professor, what exactly do Danebridge have to do to stay up?'

Mark pulled a face, but went along with the game. He could never resist having an audience.

'Well, listeners, it's basically quite simple,' he began. 'Danebridge have a superior goal difference to both their rivals, so only need another point to make certain of survival. And they could even afford to lose against Selworth so long as Ashford didn't win their game. Now this is where it starts to get really interesting mathematically – because if Ashford . . .'

Rakesh snatched the microphone away quickly. 'Yes, thank you, Professor. Very interesting, I'm sure, but that's all we have time for at the moment. Now over to the weather forecast . . .'

'Anyway, it's no use thinking about what Ashford might do,' said Chris. 'They're playing on Saturday as well so we won't even know their result.'

'Yes, we will,' Mark grinned. 'My dad will be there. He's going to keep ringing Mum on the mobile to relay the score.'

'Tell him he needn't bother, 'cos we're gonna thrash Selworth,' Rakesh boasted. 'I've promised them a hat-trick!'

The captain wished he could be so optimistic. Selworth had already beaten Danebridge 5–1, their heaviest defeat of the season.

5 *On the Attack*

'I've been thinking,' said Chris as the players went over the footbridge onto the recky for their regular Thursday practice session. 'It's a bit like when I fell off that pony.'

Philip paused to gaze down into the rippling water of the river below to see if he could spot any fish. He couldn't. He never did, but he always stopped to look. 'What – still sore, you mean?'

'No! Are you listening? I'm talking about our poor form in the league.'

'Yeah, right . . . er . . . why is that like falling off a pony?'

'Well, we've got to pick ourselves up and try to do better, just like I had to last week,' Chris explained.

'We sure need to play a lot better this time against Selworth. A draw's about the best we can hope for, I reckon.'

'Maybe, but it's too risky just playing for a draw. It could be curtains if they went and scored a late goal to beat us,' Chris said. 'We've got to be positive and go there looking for a win.'

Mr Jones must have agreed. He set up one of their favourite practice games – attack versus defence. The attackers earned points for every effort at goal, plus a bonus if they scored, while the defenders gained points for clearing the ball over the halfway line.

The defence was soon on top. They built up a useful early lead and made

the attacking players work hard to create any decent chances. Rakesh had the first shot on target, but saw it deflected away by Philip for a corner. Ryan took it, swinging the ball into the goalmouth where Chris leapt high to snatch it clean off Rakesh's head.

Heading was not their strong point. The strikers were all small, nippy players who preferred having the ball at their feet rather than up in the air. They had little hope of outjumping tall defenders and goalkeepers. The next swift attack, however, provided a perfect example of their strengths.

Ryan and Rakesh exchanged neat passes to carve open the defence before Rakesh slipped the ball through to Kerry. It was a killer pass. Left with just Philip to beat, Kerry almost tied his long legs in knots as she dummied one way and then the other. He had no idea what she was going to do next.

Neither did Chris. When the shot was finally unleashed, it caught him

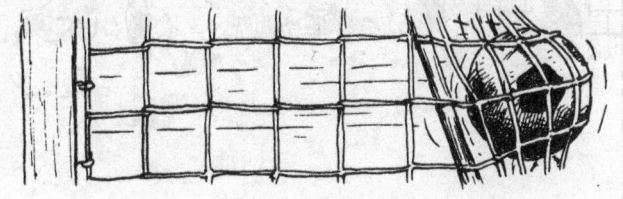

wrong-footed and the keeper could only watch the ball whizz past into the goal. In a sense, he was pleased. It was good to see Kerry so sharp again – and it was great to have Rakesh back too. They were going to need them both on top form on Saturday.

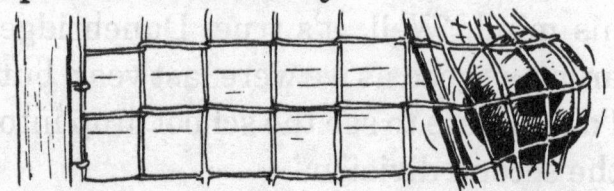

'Good luck, our kid,' said Andrew as he and Chris clambered out of Grandad's car outside Selworth School. 'Hope Danebridge stay up.'

'Do you really mean that?'

'Course I do.'

'But you've been taunting me all season about us getting relegated, just like Luke. You've made it sound like you really want it to happen.'

Andrew grinned. 'Nah, you know

me. Only pulling your leg.'

'C'mon, be honest. I bet you'll be secretly pleased if we go down, just so you can say the team's rubbish since you left.'

Andrew's grin turned somewhat sheepish, knowing that Chris had read his mind. 'Well, it's true, Danebridge aren't as good as we were last year, but I'd still hate to see the school drop into the second division.'

Grandad interrupted. 'Anyway, whatever happens today, it's not the end of the world.'

'It's not even the end of the season,' Chris added. 'We've still got a big cup match to play next week, remember.'

'Just make sure your team concentrate on this one first,' Grandad chuckled. 'You know what they say in football – take each game as it comes.'

Danebridge started this game in great style. After mounting a series of

dangerous attacks, the Reds put the
ball in the Selworth net.

'What a goal!' cried Rakesh. 'Keeper
never moved!'

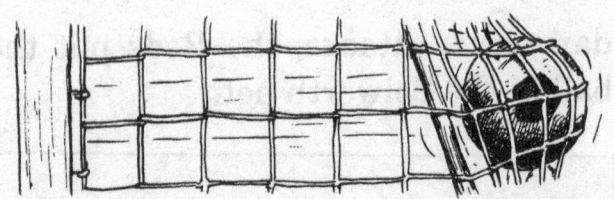

His delight was short-lived. He'd just leapt onto the scorer's back, toppling Ryan to the ground, when the referee's repeated blasts on the whistle made him realize that something was wrong.

'No goal,' announced Selworth's teacher. 'Free-kick to the Blues.'

Rakesh scrambled to his feet first and stared at the referee in disbelief. He hadn't seen any foul before Ryan crashed the ball home, and nobody could have been offside. A defender had been standing on the goal line.

'Sorry, Rakesh,' said the referee. 'It was handball.'

If it had been anyone else, Rakesh might have made a protest, but he knew the referee well. Mr Carter had once been his class teacher.

Ryan confirmed the decision was correct. 'He's right, Rakky,' he admitted. 'The ball bounced up and hit my hand before I shot.'

Five minutes later, the visitors suffered a further setback. There was a goal at the other end, and this one counted. Danebridge failed to clear a corner properly and the ball was stabbed past Chris from close range.

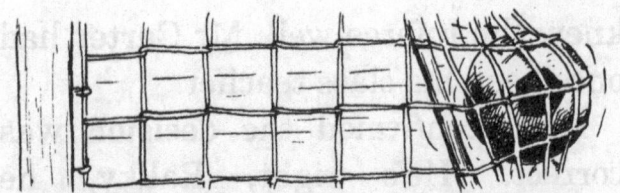

What made it worse for Rakesh was that the scorer was his best mate at Selworth, a lad that he still played with for a Sunday League side. After his noisy celebrations, Dinesh made sure that he caught his friend's eye.

'Wicked goal, eh, Rakky?' he cackled.

'Huh! Goalhanging, as usual,' Rakesh retorted, unimpressed. 'We'll see who has the last laugh.'

There wasn't much for Danebridge to laugh about in the first half.

Ryan and Kerry hit good chances over the bar, Rakesh hooked another into the side netting and Mark had to limp off with a leg injury. The mood in the camp at half-time would have been even more grim-faced, if Chris hadn't pulled off two super saves to prevent Selworth adding to their 1–0 lead.

The only thing that cheered them up a little was the news coming through from the other game. Mark had taken charge of the phone.

'Don't worry, Dad says Ashford are losing too,' he announced. 'They kicked off before us and they're 2–1 behind in the second half.'

'Er . . . can we be sure your dad's right about the score?' Chris said hesitantly. 'I mean, you've often told us he gets numbers the wrong way round and stuff like that.'

'Surprised he even knows what number to dial,' added Rakesh. 'He's got a worse memory than you, Professor.'

Mark looked hurt, wishing his mum hadn't said anything about Dad forgetting to take the phone with him that morning. He'd driven halfway to Ashford before returning home to collect it.

'The phone does have a built-in memory system, y'know,' he sneered in reply. 'If you've ever used one.'

'Yeah, but has it got a calculator as well?'

As Mr Jones attempted to start his team talk, the phone rang and Mark clamped it to his ear. 'Hi, Dad . . . There's been another goal? Great! Is that 3–1 now? . . .'

Their hopes rose as they listened to Mark's end of the conversation.

'. . . Oh! You mean Ashford got it . . .'

Their faces fell.

'Sorry, guys,' Mark said with a shrug. 'Seems they've just gone and equalized. It's two–all there now.'

6 Wrong Numbers

As the teams lined up for the second half, Chris gazed around the crowded touchline. He had never seen so many Danebridge supporters at an away match before. But then, of course, this was no ordinary match. Their place in the league was at stake.

One particular person, however, was nowhere in sight and Chris was very glad about that. 'Bradshaw's face when everybody refused to bring him here this morning!' he chuckled to himself at the memory. 'Classic!'

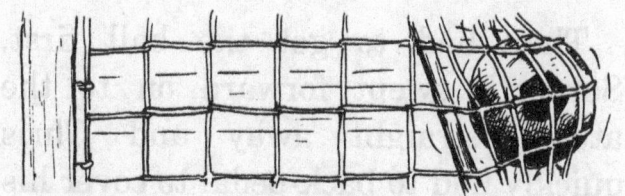

Chris had glanced out of the rear window as they drove off, just to check that Luke Bradshaw had been unsuccessful in cadging a lift. The outcast was standing alone on the pavement, snarling with fury at being left behind by the convoy of cars heading for Selworth.

'Get stuck in, Reds! Go for goals.'

Andrew's loud, clear voice carried across the pitch and snapped his younger brother's mind back into focus on the task in hand. Chris instantly forgot all about Luke Bradshaw.

'C'mon, team,' the captain yelled from the edge of his penalty area as Selworth kicked off. 'Big effort! Let's play them off the park.'

They had to get the ball first. Selworth swept forward on to the attack straight away and Chris quickly had to back-pedal to cover his goal.

'Mark up, defence,' he cried. 'Watch that number eight, Phil.'

Dinesh was the striker in question and he was proving a real handful for Philip, especially when the ball was on the ground. On this occasion, the winger sent over a high cross, which was far more to the centre-back's liking. He would give a giraffe a good contest in the air.

Philip's head met the ball firmly, clearing it well out of the penalty area to where Ryan was hovering. He linked up with Rakesh on the halfway line and a clever one-two sent Rakesh away, running deep into Selworth territory.

The winger had the speed and skill to take on two blue shirts and dribble past them before drilling the ball low into the goalmouth. Kerry's lightning strike was unstoppable. There was a flash of red and white at the near post and the ball was in the net.

'The equalizer!' cried Rakesh. 'Brilliant flick, Kez.'

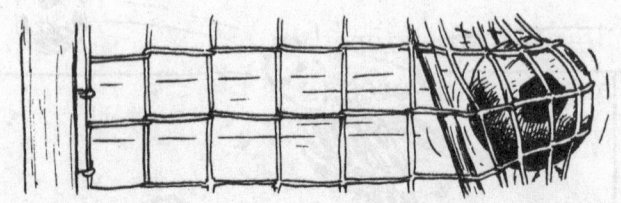

'One goal's not enough,' Kerry insisted, staying calm. 'We can't relax yet. We need another.'

Andrew grew more confident as he watched Danebridge take control and play their best football of the match. 'Just a matter of time before we score again,' he predicted. 'We're well on top now.'

Grandad shook his head. 'Don't count your chickens. A game's not over until the final whistle. You soon learn that in football, m'boy.'

The one at Ashford blew well in advance of Mr Carter's. The players soon became aware of that when they saw Mark jumping up and down in excitement, despite his bad leg. Mr

Jones had ordered him not to give out any more scores, but he just couldn't contain himself.

'The goals were really flying in at the end,' he shouted. 'Finished 4–3.'

'Who to?' demanded Rakesh. 'That's what we want to know.'

'Er . . . hold on, I can't quite make it out. The line's breaking up and I think Dad must be standing near a lot of people. They're all cheering . . .'

Andrew charged up to him. 'C'mon, who won, you nutter?' he screamed at Mark in frustration. 'Ashford or Highgate?'

'Er . . . not sure – Dad sounded a bit confused. Sorry.'

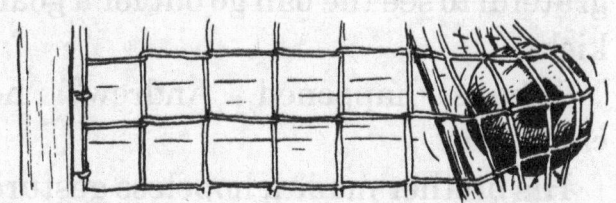

'Sorry! Is that all you can say?'

Mark shrugged and lowered the phone helplessly. 'Got cut off. Line's gone dead. The battery must be flat or something . . .'

His voice trailed away, half afraid that Andrew was going to hit him. The Danebridge team had virtually stopped playing, distracted by the drama on the touchline.

'Watch out!' shouted the headmaster. 'They're coming at us.'

His warning was almost too late. Philip stirred himself just in time to put in a challenge and make the attacker slice his shot against the post. Chris was nowhere near it and was grateful to see the ball go out for a goal-kick.

'What's happened, Andrew?' he called out.

His brother made a hopeless gesture

with his hands. 'Dunno. The mad professor and his dad have messed up. Best to assume Ashford have won. You've got to hang on for the draw now or you've had it.'

Rakesh ran up to the referee. 'How long to go, Mr Carter?'

The teacher glanced at his stop-watch. 'About five minutes yet.'

For the Danebridge players and supporters, those last few minutes were a slow, agonizing torture. They seemed more like five endless hours. One mistake now could send them down.

And there were lots of them. Panic set in and Selworth took advantage of their opponents' jitters. They pressed

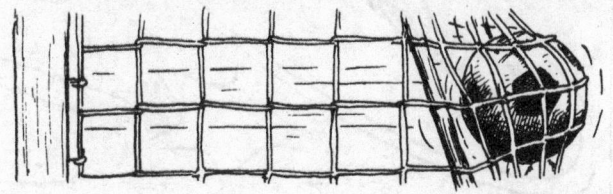

forward eagerly, sensing victory, and the Danebridge goal led a charmed life. Philip headed one effort off the line and another skimmed just wide of the upright.

When the ball fell to the feet of Dinesh inside the final minute of the game, however, the goal was at his mercy. Only Chris stood between the

striker and an inviting expanse of netting. The keeper flung himself recklessly into the line of fire and felt the shot slam into his body. He had no idea where the ball went to after that, apart from the fact that it didn't go past him.

Dinesh could hardly believe that he hadn't scored the winner. 'How did you stop that one?' he gasped.

'Luck mostly, I think,' Chris replied, shaking his head. 'I just had to get in the way of it.'

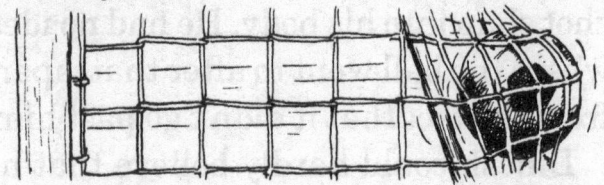

As applause echoed around the pitch for the magnificent save, the referee checked his watch again and the game moved into added time. There were only a few seconds left now for Danebridge to hold on.

Kerry gained possession of the ball near the right touchline and decided to run with it towards the corner flag in a bid to use up some valuable time. Two defenders tracked her down but with a shimmy and a wiggle, she was free and a path to goal suddenly opened up in front of her. It was too tempting to resist.

Two strange things happened then. The first was that Kerry opted to pass rather than shoot, a rare event in itself, and the second was that Rakesh headed the ball.

The shooting angle was too tight even for Kerry to think she could score and she whipped over a cross instead about waist height. Rakesh met it with a superb diving header at the far post, his body horizontal with the ground. He made contact with the ball a fraction before a defender's boot did so against his face.

The ball was in the net, the

Danebridge players were celebrating and the referee signalled the end of the match, but Rakesh was still lying flat out in the goalmouth. As his team-mates helped the dazed scorer to sit up, they saw that his shirt was redder than anyone else's. Blood was dripping from his nose.

'Fantastic header, Rakky!' cried Ryan. 'We've won!'

'Have to get you cleaned up,' Kerry smiled. 'Looks like you've been in another fight with Luke.'

Rakesh managed a lopsided grin. 'Worth it. Feels even better to win this one – the fight against relegation!'

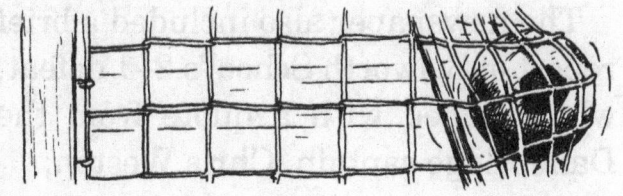

Monday's edition of the *Selworth Mail* printed a copy of the final league table, confirming Ashford's dramatic 4–3 victory that sent unlucky Brentway sinking into Division 2.

Bottom three places . . .							
					Goals		
	P	W	D	L	F	A	Pts
Danebridge	16	4	4	8	24	33	16
Ashford	16	4	3	9	27	42	15
Brentway	16	3	5	8	20	38	14

The newspaper also included a brief report of Selworth School's 2–1 defeat, which ended with a quote from the Danebridge captain, Chris Weston:

'We just take each game as it comes. Now we're safe, we can't wait to play our next big match – the semi-final of the cup!'

THE END

ABOUT THE AUTHOR

Rob Childs was born and grew up in Derby. His childhood ambition was to become an England cricketer or footballer – preferably both! After university, however, he went into teaching and taught in primary and high schools in Leicestershire, where he now lives. Always interested in school sports, he coached school teams and clubs across a range of sports, and ran area representative teams in football, cricket and athletics.

Recognizing a need for sports fiction for young readers, he decided to have a go at writing such stories himself and now has more than fifty books to his name, including the popular *The Big Match* series, published by Young Corgi Books.

Rob has now left teaching in order to be able to write full-time. Married to Joy, also a writer, Rob has a 'lassie' dog called Laddie and is also a keen photographer.

THE BIG FIX
Rob Childs

'Offside, ref!'
'Play on!' bellowed the referee . . .

Danebridge football team, captained by
goalkeeper Chris Weston, face an uphill
struggle when they meet their local
rivals, Shenby, in a cup-tie. For the
referee – Shenby's new sports teacher –
might as well be *playing* for Shenby. *All*
his decisions go their way!

Can Chris, with the help of his brother,
Andrew, find a way of making sure their
next match against Shenby – a vital
league clash – will be a fair one? Or will
Danebridge's cup *and* league hopes be
dashed because of a biased referee . . . ?

ISBN 0 552 545341

YOUNG CORGI BOOKS

THE BIG FREEZE
Rob Childs

'Bottom of the table!' moaned Pud.
'We've got no chance of qualifying for the
Final now.'

The big freeze is wrecking the team's
soccer season – they haven't played a
proper match for two months and the
novelty of playing indoors has
long worn off.

But then Jamie's father books them in
for sessions on the all-weather pitches
at the new sports centre, and they find
themselves taking part in an exciting
triangular tournament. But will Pud be
able to keep his feet on the unfamiliar
surface? And will the big-headed Carl
Diamond keep them out of the Final?

ISBN 0 552 52967 2

YOUNG CORGI BOOKS

SOCCER MAD

Rob Childs

*'This is going to be the match of
the century!'*

Luke Crawford is crazy about football. A
walking encyclopedia of football facts
and trivia, he throws his enthusiasm
into being captain of the Swillsby
Swifts, a Sunday team make up mostly
of boys like himself – boys who love
playing football but get few chances to
play in real matches.

Luke is convinced that good teamwork
and plenty of practice can turn his side
into winners on the pitch, but he faces a
real challenge when the Swifts are
drawn to play the Padley Panthers – the
league stars – in the first round of the
Sunday League Cup . . .

ISBN 0 440 86344 9

CORGI YEARLING BOOKS

All Transworld titles can be ordered by post from:

Book Service By Post, PO Box 29, Douglas, Isle of Man, IM99 1BQ

Credit cards accepted. Please telephone 01624 675137
fax 01624 670923, Internet http://www.bookpost.co.uk
or e-mail: bookshop@enterprise.net for details

Free postage and packing in the UK. Overseas customers: allow £1 per
book (paperbacks) and £3 per book (hardbacks).